Text copyright © 1973 by Bernice Chardiet Illustrations copyright © 1973 by Hope Meryman All rights reserved. First published in the United States of America in 1973 by the Walker Publishing Company, Inc. Published simultaneously in Canada by Fitzhenry & White-side, Limited, Toronto Trade ISBN: 0-8027-6155-0 Reinf ISBN: 0-8027-6156-9 Library of Congress Catalog Card Number: 73-81783 Printed in the United States of America.

Juan Bobo
and The Pig

A Puerto Rican Folktale Retold

BY BERNICE CHARDIET

ILLUSTRATED BY HOPE MERYMAN

WALKER AND COMPANY
New York

a Puerto Rico, que con su
belleza y tradiciones ha
inspirado estos cuentos
y
a mi esposo, Oscar Chardiet de la Torre,
que me ha hecho amar la cultura Latino-Americana.

Once upon a time, in a small village high in the
mountains, there lived a poor, old widow.

The widow had a son named Juan. But he was such
a ninny and did such silly things that everyone called
him Juan Bobo—or John the Boob.

For a while, when Juan Bobo was little, his mother would say to him, "Ay, Juan! If only you would think more."

But she soon saw that the more Juan thought, the more trouble he got into.

So then she said, "Ay, Juan! If only you would think less." And this pleased Juan Bobo very much.

One day, Juan Bobo's mother called him in from the field and said, "Now, Juan, I am going to the church for a while. You had better stay inside the house and take care of the animals. Don't start thinking and getting into trouble while I am gone—eh?"

"Don't worry, Mama," said Juan Bobo. "I will do just as you say."

And he went inside the house and sat down without thinking.

But soon he heard the pig oinking in the yard. "I wonder why the pig is oinking?" thought Juan Bobo. And he went outside to see.

"What's the matter with you?" he asked the pig.
"The minute Mama leaves you start making trouble. What
do you want?"

"Oink, Oink," went the pig.

"What kind of an answer is that?" Juan Bobo asked.
"How do I know what you want if all you do is oink?"

The pig oinked again.

"If you won't talk," Juan Bobo said, "I will have
to guess."

And Juan Bobo began to think.

"The pig is not hungry," he thought. "Mama fed him
before she left. The pig is not sleepy," he thought.
"He just had a nap."

Now the pig was ready. Juan Bobo carried him outside and put him down in the road.

"You will have to find the way by yourself. I have to stay home," he told the pig. "Run along—and come back with Mama."

Juan Bobo looked at the pig. "I know why you are oinking," Juan Bobo said. "You are lonesome for Mama. You want to go to church and be with her, don't you?"

"Well, you can't go!" Juan Bobo told the pig. "You have to be all dressed up to go to church. So just forget about it, and stop making noise."

But then, Juan Bobo felt sorry for the pig. So he said, "All right. You can go. But first you will have to be properly dressed."

And he took the pig inside the house.

Juan Bobo opened the chest of drawers where his mother kept her things. In the bottom drawer, he found two dresses. Carefully, he picked out the best one and put it on the pig.

In the middle drawer, he found a lace mantilla. He tied it around the pig's head.

In the top drawer, he found a string of pearls his mother had worn for her wedding. He hung them pig's neck.

Next to the pearls, he found the pair of golde earrings his mother wore on feast days. He put the pig's ears.

Last, he found his mother's slippers and pu on the pig's hind feet.

And he went inside the house and closed the door.
As soon as the pig found out he was alone, he
kicked off the slippers and began to run.

And he went inside the house and closed the door.
As soon as the pig found out he was alone, he
kicked off the slippers and began to run.

Juan Bobo looked at the pig. "I know why you are oinking," Juan Bobo said. "You are lonesome for Mama. You want to go to church and be with her, don't you?"

"Well, you can't go!" Juan Bobo told the pig. "You have to be all dressed up to go to church. So just forget about it, and stop making noise."

But then, Juan Bobo felt sorry for the pig. So he said, "All right. You can go. But first you will have to be properly dressed."

And he took the pig inside the house.

Now the pig was ready. Juan Bobo carried him
outside and put him down in the road.

"You will have to find the way by yourself. I have
to stay home," he told the pig. "Run along—and come
back with Mama."

Juan Bobo opened the chest of drawers where his mother kept her things. In the bottom drawer, he found two dresses. Carefully, he picked out the best one and put it on the pig.

In the middle drawer, he found a lace mantilla. He tied it around the pig's head.

In the top drawer, he found a string of pearls his mother had worn for her wedding. He hung them around the pig's neck.

Next to the pearls, he found the pair of golden earrings his mother wore on feast days. He put them in the pig's ears.

Last, he found his mother's slippers and put them on the pig's hind feet.

"Oh, that naughty pig!" Juan Bobo said. "He must have kicked them off. Maybe they were too tight."

"Too tight? What do you mean?" his mother asked. "What was the pig doing out in the road in my slippers?"

Juan Bobo said, "He was lonesome so I dressed him and sent him to church. Didn't you see him there?"

"You did what?" Juan's mother shouted. "You simpleton! Just wait, you blockhead you! I'll teach you a lesson. I'll give you a spanking you'll never forget!"

And she rushed out of the house to look for the pig.

By the time she reached the pond, the angry pig had
torn off the clothes and was just biting the last piece
of the mantilla to bits.

Juan Bobo's mother tied the pig up with a rope and
led him back to the yard.

He ran straight to a muddy pond, nearby, and threw himself in. He rolled over and over, wriggling and thrashing about— trying to fight his way out of his clothes.

A little while later, Juan Bobo's mother came home.
She wondered why her slippers were out in the road. She
took them inside and asked Juan Bobo about them.

Then, true to her word, she went inside and gave
Juan Bobo the spanking of his life to teach him a
lesson.

Juan Bobo never forgot that spanking.

But what was the lesson? He could not remember.